Eric Craig

New Zealand Ferns

Eric Craig

New Zealand Ferns

ISBN/EAN: 9783741198526

Manufactured in Europe, USA, Canada, Australia, Japa

Cover: Foto ©Andreas Hilbeck / pixelio.de

Manufactured and distributed by brebook publishing software
(www.brebook.com)

Eric Craig

New Zealand Ferns

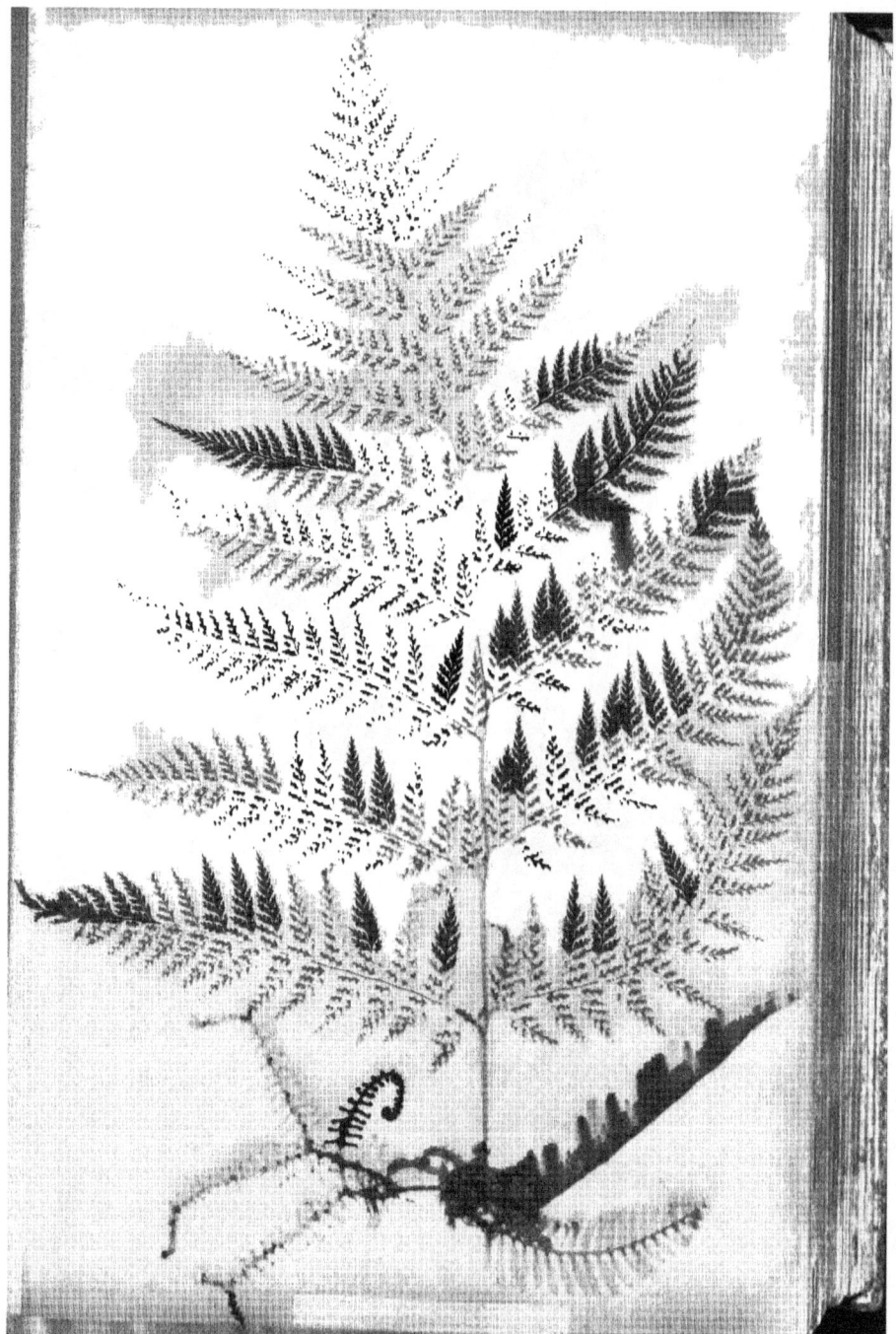

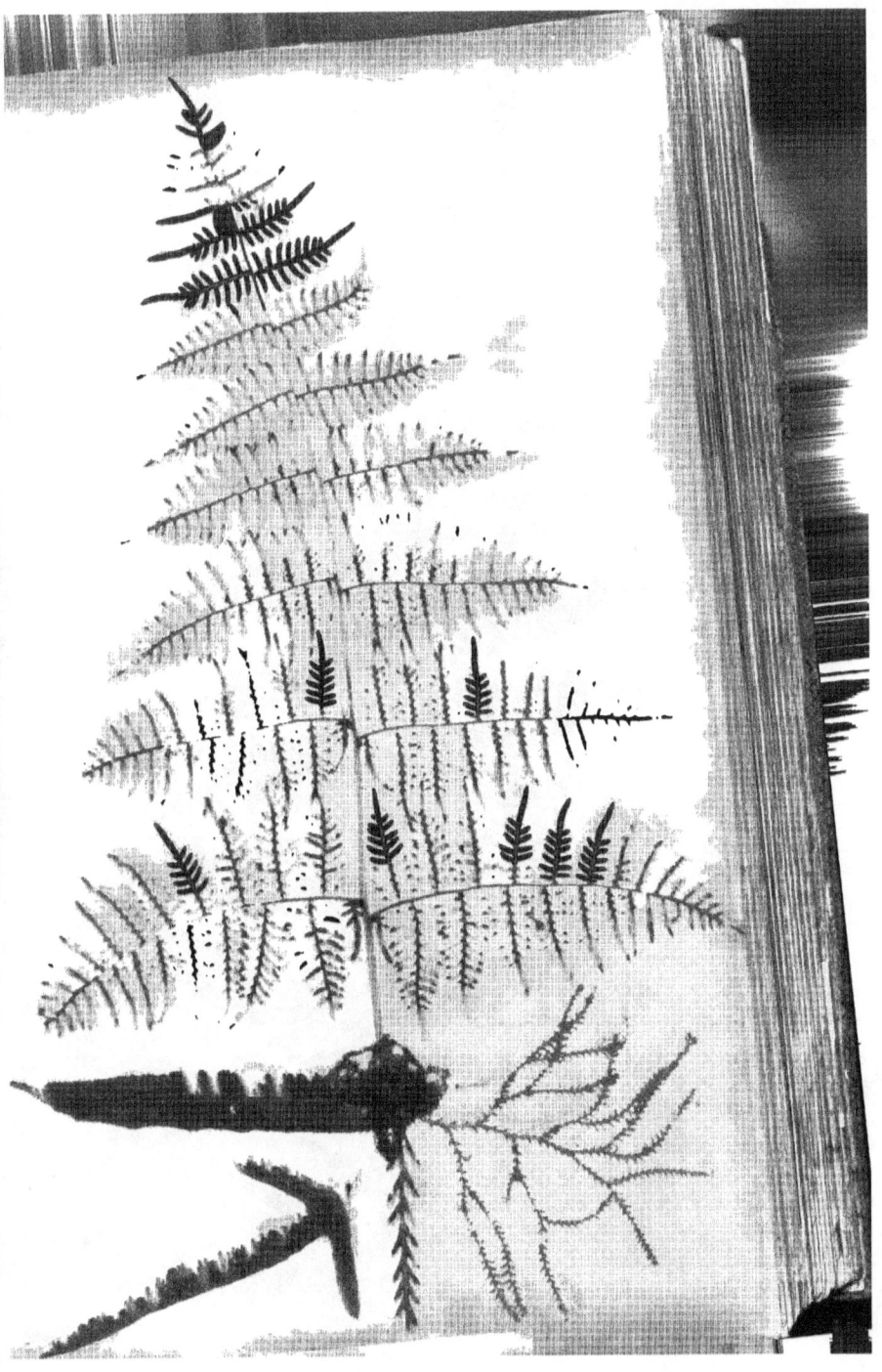

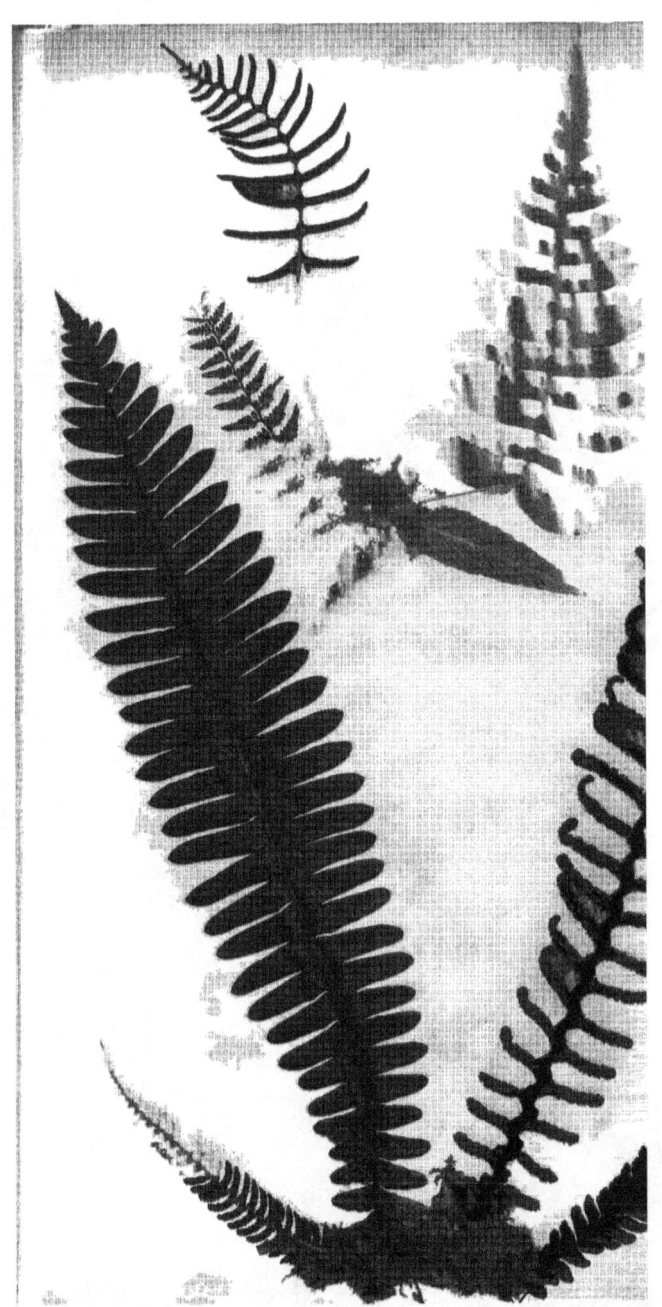

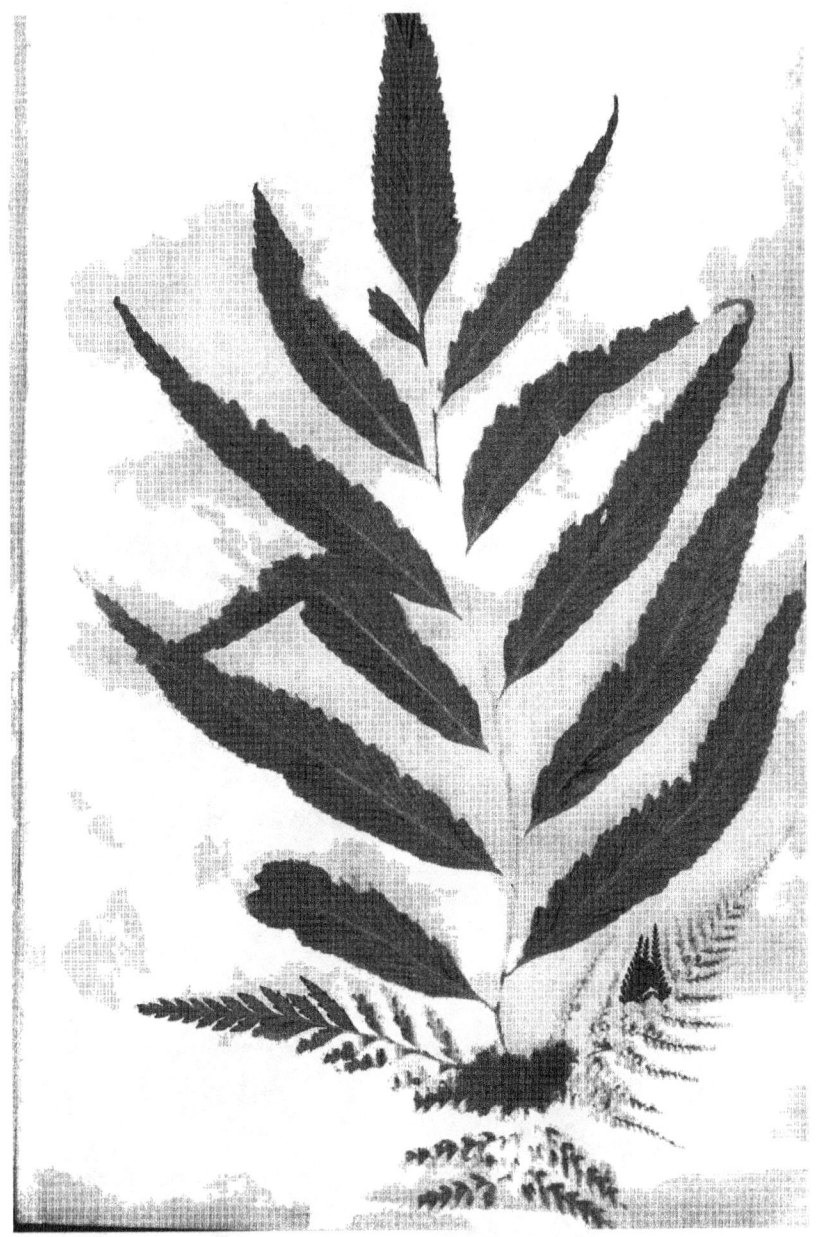

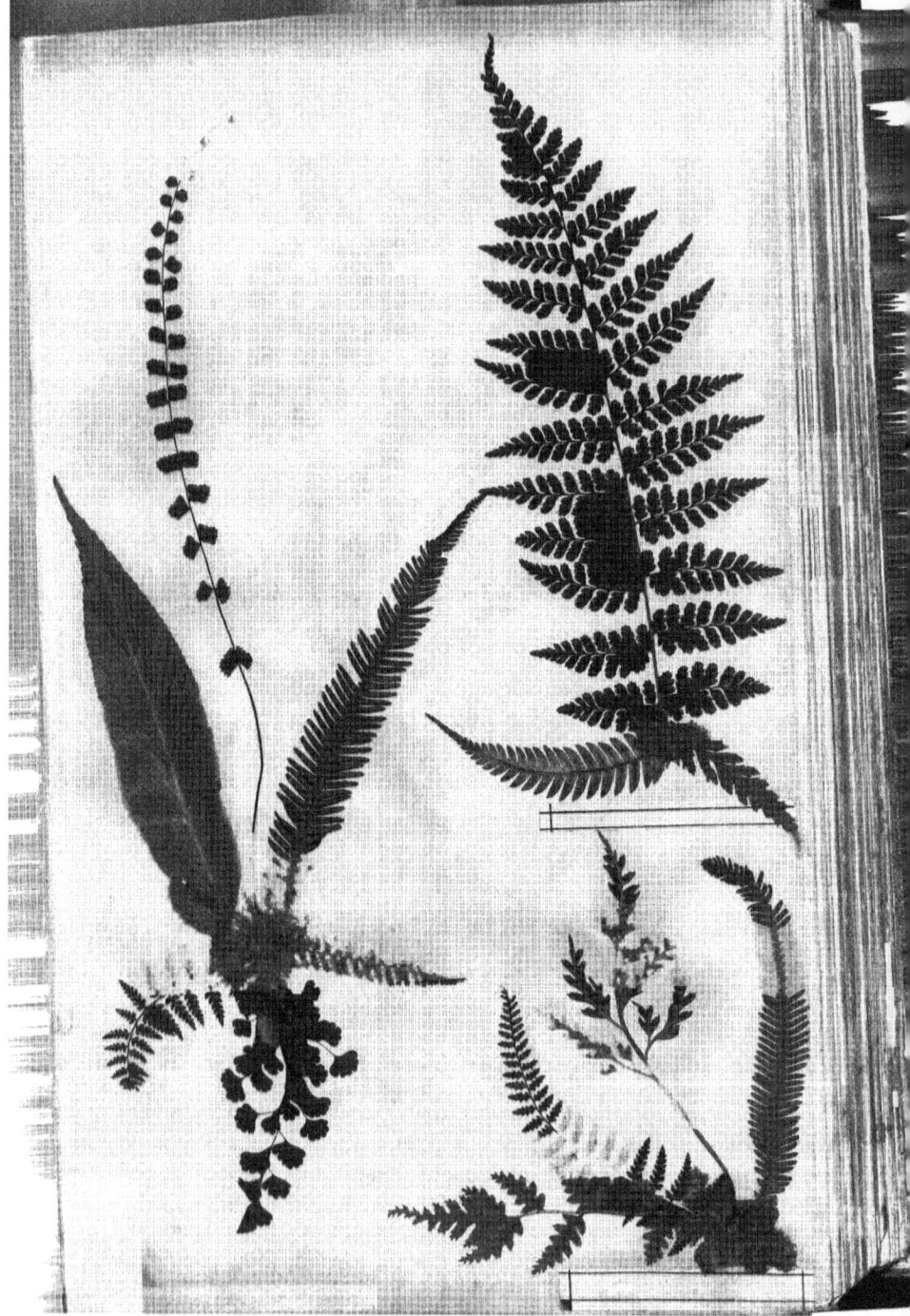

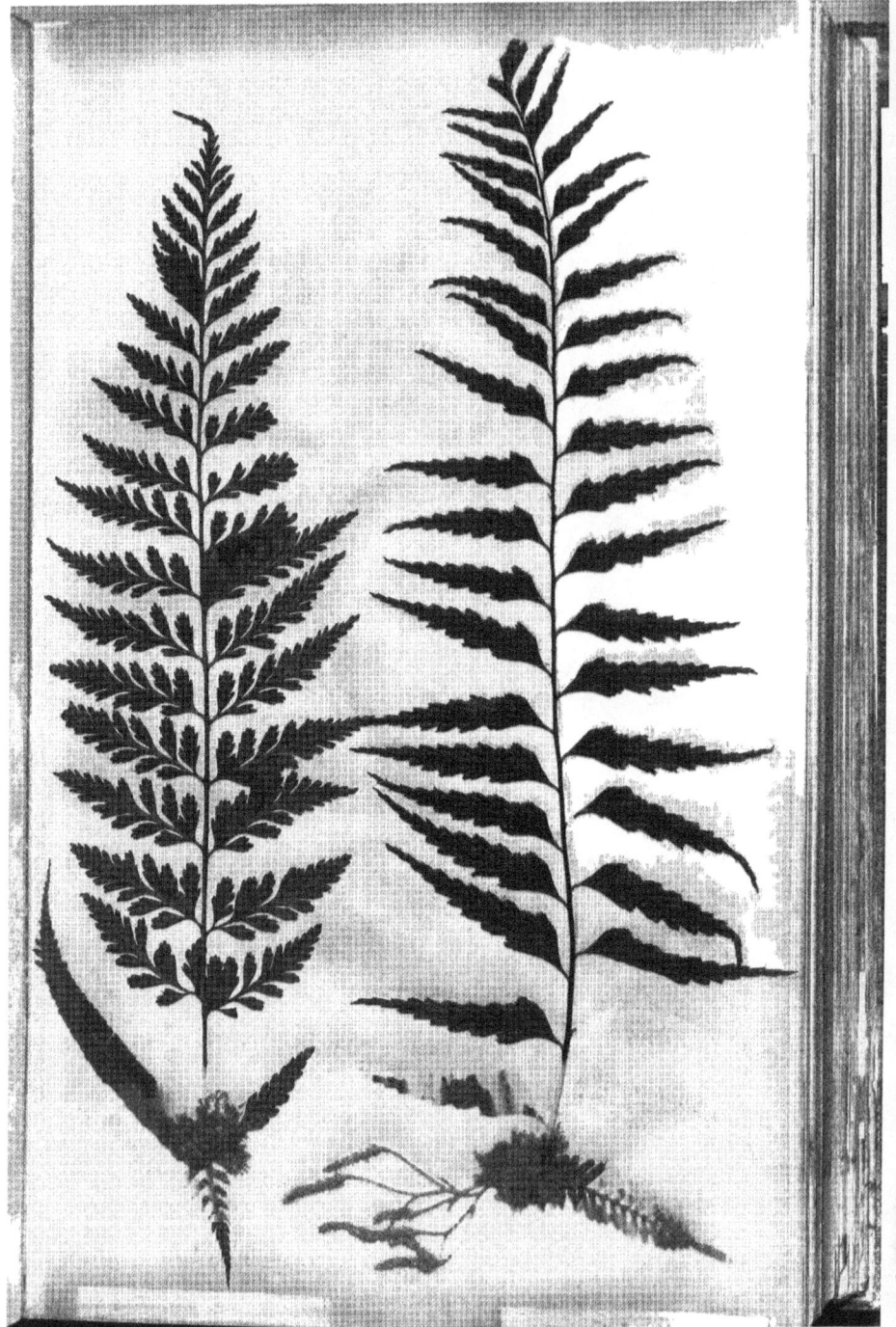

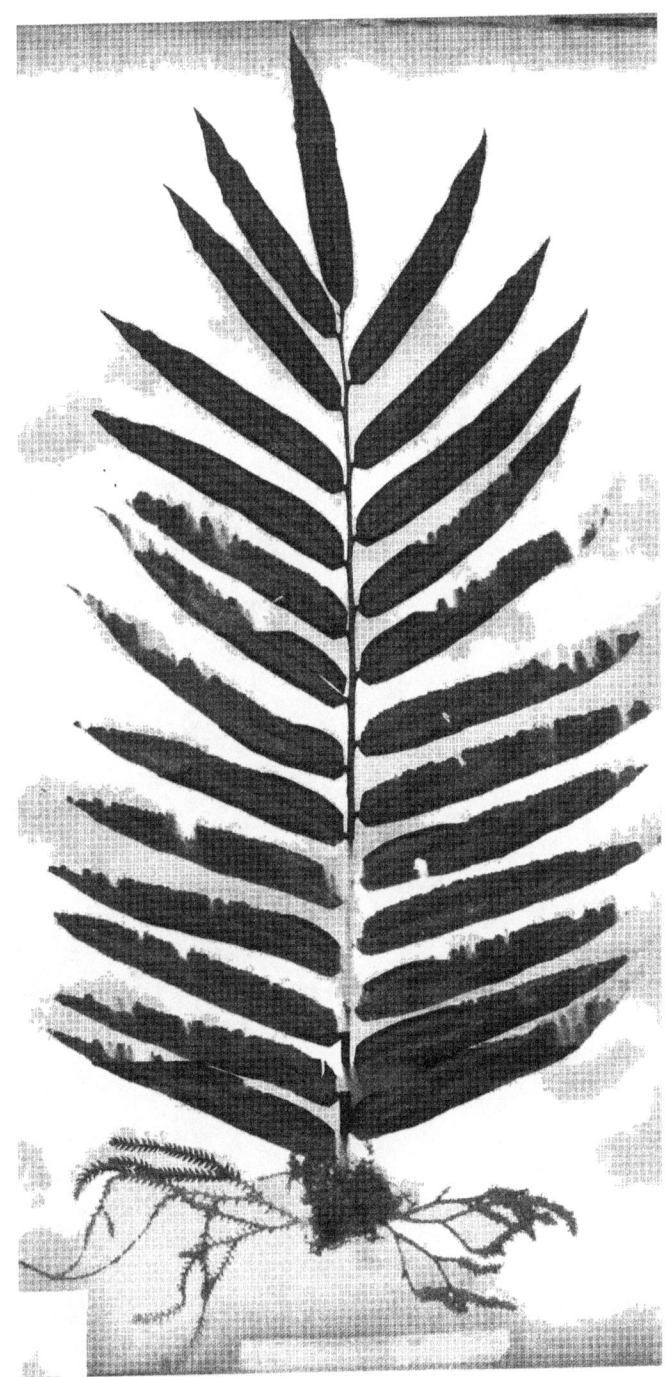

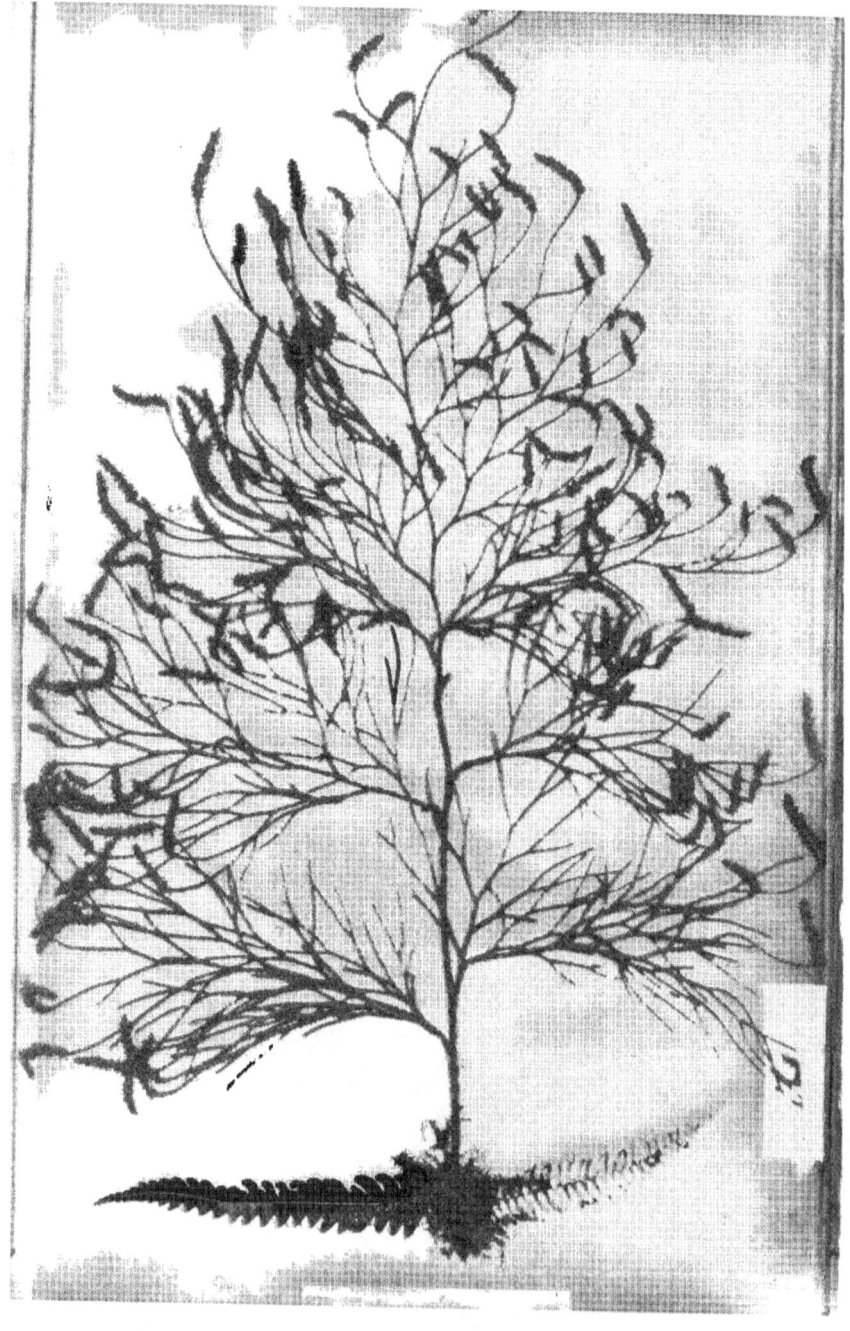

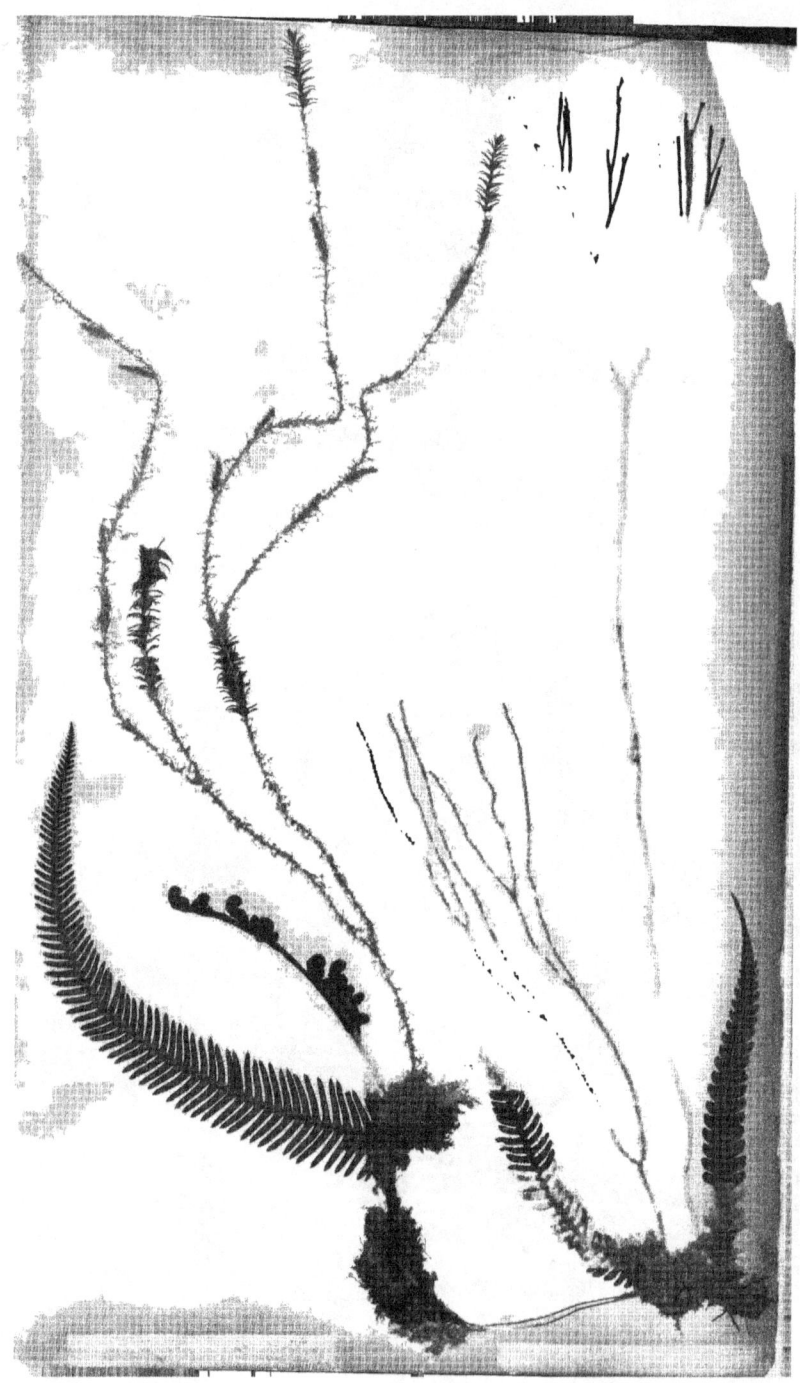